MAGGIE SPARKS

First published in the UK by Sweet Cherry Publishing Limited, 2023
Unit 36, Vulcan House, Vulcan Road,
Leicester, LE5 3EF, United Kingdom

Sweet Cherry Europe (Europe address)
Nauschgasse 4/3/2 POB 1017
Vienna, WI 1220, Austria

2 4 6 8 10 9 7 5 3 1

ISBN: 978-1-78226-717-1

Maggie Sparks and the Alien Invasion

Text © Steve Smallman, 2023
Illustration © Sweet Cherry Publishing Limited, 2023

Illustrations by Esther Hernando

www.sweetcherrypublishing.com

Printed and bound in India

MAGGIE SPÁRKS

AND THE
ALIEN INVASION

STEVE SMALLMAN

ILLUSTRATED BY
ESTHER HERNANDO

Sweet
Cherry

MAGGIE
That's me!

BAT
The coolest chameleon EVER.

MUM
Super smart.
Bakes great cookies.

DAD
Writes a lot.
Cannot bake cookies.

ALFIE
Stinky and
annoying.

GRANDAD
My favourite
wizard in the world!

ARTHUR
My best friend.

CHAPTER 1

Maggie Sparks was a witch. A small, curly-haired, freckle-faced witch, who was usually full of mischief and fizzing with

MAGIC.

But today she wasn't *just* a witch ...

she was a space witch from the
planet ASTRO-CADABRA!
Her pet chameleon, Bat, was now a
three-eyed alien swamp lizard.

A strange spaceship had just
landed. Arthur, the space explorer,
was climbing out of it.

'PING PONG, SWIRLY BLEEP!'
shouted Maggie.

'What?' asked Arthur.

'I was talking in an alien language,' whispered Maggie. 'I said "Hello, earthling".'

'Oh, right. Hello, space witch!' said Arthur. 'I have travelled thousands of light years to get here ...'

'Do you need a wee?' said Maggie.

'No,' said Arthur.

'Are you sure?' giggled Maggie. 'I usually need a wee after a long journey.'

'Actually,' huffed Arthur, 'it was a VERY long journey. It was so long that I had to travel in a cryogenic pod.'

'A crying what?' said Maggie.

'A cry-o-gen-ic pod,' said Arthur.

'It freezes you, so you can travel for years without getting any older.'

'Oh, like peas!' said Maggie. 'They sit in a pod and get frozen, so they stay fresh for ages. You're a pea, Arthur. A pea in a spacesuit!'

Then Maggie laughed so much she got hiccups.

Arthur took off his space helmet and threw it on the floor. 'You're spoiling the game!' he shouted.

'Sorry … hic!' said Maggie. 'But – HIC – that was funny!'

Arthur didn't think it was funny at all. He stomped off home.

'What's wrong with him?' Maggie asked Bat. 'He's no fun anymore.'

Bat shrugged his shoulders and pulled off his extra "eye" (a ping-pong ball on a straw).

Arthur was Maggie's best friend,
even though they were nothing alike.

Arthur was quiet.
Maggie was noisy.

Arthur was tidy.
Maggie was messy.

Arthur was
nervous. Maggie
was bold.

Arthur was sensible. Maggie was, well, not.

The biggest difference between them was **MAGIC.** Maggie was a witch and there was nothing magical about Arthur.

But lately, Arthur had changed.

'It's all because of that stupid science club,' said Maggie.

Arthur LOVED science. His favourite time of the whole week was Thursday's after-school science club. Maggie went too, but it was NOT her favourite thing to do. Especially not now that Arthur had met Freddy, Tanek and Lily. They all LOVED science too!

Arthur talked to his new friends about plants and planets and telescopes and stuff. Maggie didn't understand what they were talking about some of the time. The rest of the time, she didn't listen. She felt left out.

'What can I do, Bat?' said Maggie. 'Arthur and I have always been the odd ones out at school. But now Arthur has his science friends, so the only odd one out is … me.'

Bat sighed and turned blue (he always did when Maggie felt sad or lonely).

'Maybe if I knew lots of facts about science, I might fit in with his new friends,' said Maggie.

Bat nodded. He rummaged through Maggie's bookshelf and

pulled out *1001 Fascinating Facts for the Young Scientist*.

'Brilliant!' said Maggie. 'I'm not going to move until I've learnt every fact in this book. I don't care how long it takes.'

Maggie started reading.

A whole three minutes later, she cried, 'I give up! This is SOOOOOO boring!'

Maggie stomped downstairs, grumpy and out of ideas. She would NEVER fit in with Arthur's new friends. She would never fit in with ANYONE.

'Maggie,' said Mum, 'have you got everything ready for your trip to the space centre tomorrow?'

'Tomorrow?' gasped Maggie. She had forgotten all about it.

Miss Raven had arranged for the science club to visit a space centre. Arthur had been looking forward to it for ages. It was perfect timing. Maggie could show Arthur and his new friends just how sensible and quiet and totally interested in space she could be.

What could go wrong?

Maggie came down for breakfast the next morning with a spring in her step.

'What are you wearing, Maggie?' asked Mum.

'My super space outfit!' said Maggie.
'You look great,' said Dad. 'But
why are you not wearing your school
uniform?'

'Miss Raven told us to wear our own clothes and be easy to spot,' said Maggie. 'So I'm going to wear this as well.' Maggie pulled on a headband with a large, green, alien eyeball on top.

'Good choice,' said Mum, smiling. She looked up at the clock. 'OH NO! You should be on the bus by now. Let's go, Maggie!'

When they finally skidded into the school car park, all the other children were already on the bus. Miss Raven was standing outside of it, tapping her foot and looking at her watch.

'Sorry!' shouted Mum as they ran over.

'You almost missed the bus,' said Miss Raven. 'Maggie … what on earth are you wearing?'

'My super space outfit!' said Maggie. 'You told us to wear our own clothes and be easy to spot.'

Miss Raven shook her head. 'Not quite, Maggie. I said, "Do NOT wear your own clothes. Come in your school uniform, so you are easy to spot".'

'Oh, Maggie,' said Mum. 'Do you want me to fetch her school uniform, Miss Raven?'

'No, there isn't time. She'll have to come as she is,' said Miss Raven, hurrying Maggie onto the bus.

Everybody else, dressed smartly in their school uniforms, stared at Maggie as she climbed up the steps.

They started to laugh. *So much for "fitting in"*, thought Maggie.

Maggie looked for Arthur. Maggie and Arthur always sat next to each other … but Arthur was sitting next to Freddy.

Worse than that, Arthur was looking at her with his "disappointed face".

Maggie had to sit next to Mrs Grubb, the dinner lady, who had come to help out. 'Hello, dear,' said Mrs Grubb with a cheery smile. 'Mind you don't knock over the sick bucket!'

CHAPTER 2

When they arrived at the space centre, the children were met at the door by a man in an astronaut's spacesuit.

'Hi there! Welcome to the space centre. It's OUT OF THIS WORLD!' he boomed.

'My name is Chuck Meteor. I'll be your guide today. Being an astronaut, I know everything there is to know about space. If you have any questions, just put up your hand.'

Arthur's hand shot into the air.

'Do you have a question?' Chuck asked.

'If your name is Chuck Meteor,' said Arthur, 'why does it say "Colin Ramsbottom" on your name badge?'

'Oh, er, I must have picked up the wrong badge!' said Chuck, taking it off and tucking it into his pocket.

'Are you sure you're a real astronaut?' said Arthur.

'Of course I am!' said Chuck. 'Let's move on, shall we?'

The science club followed Chuck through a maze of display cases. Arthur and his "new friends" were interested in every tiny rock, model and picture. Maggie pretended to be interested, but really she was BORED.

Then Chuck led them all into
a small, dark room. He flicked a
switch on his spacesuit and a green
light glowed under his chin. It was
a bit spooky.

'OK, gather round, everyone,'
Chuck whispered. 'Prepare to be
amazed!'

He pressed a big red button
on the wall.

WHOOOOOSH!

A door opened to reveal an
enormous white rocket.

Everyone oohed and aahed.

'Isn't she a beauty?' said Chuck.

'This is the *actual* rocket that took the first men to the moon!'

Everyone was very impressed, except Arthur.

'It can't be!' said Arthur.

'Why not?' snapped Chuck.

'Because it's all here,' said Arthur. 'The lunar module and the fuel tanks and everything. The only bit that came back to Earth from the Apollo 11 mission was the command module.'

'He's right!' said Freddy,
Lily and Tanek together.

'Well … yes,' said Chuck.
'I *meant* to say that this is a
copy of the actual rocket.'

Maggie put up her hand.

'Yes!' said Chuck, pleased

to have a question from somebody who wasn't Arthur.

'How did the astronauts get into that tiny door?' Maggie asked. 'It looks like a cat flap!'

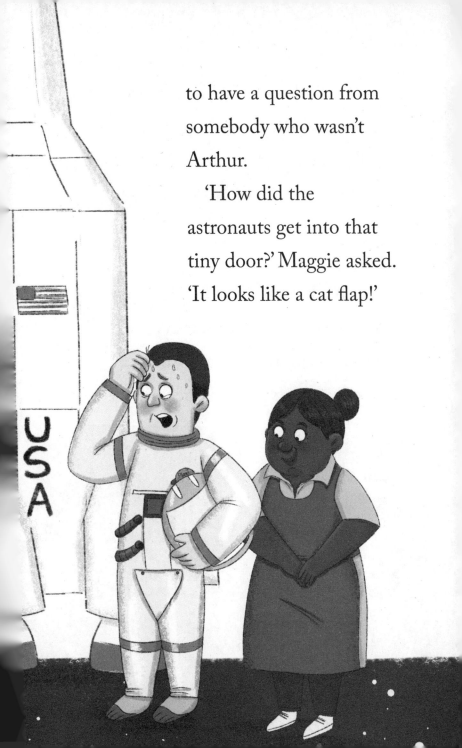

'Well, the original rocket was about twenty times bigger than this one,' said Chuck.

'So it's just a little model then,' said Maggie. 'It's not the real thing at all.'

Chuck glared at Maggie. Then he shouted, 'This way, everyone!' before walking over to a series of glass cabinets full of spacesuits.

Some were big, some were small
and there was even a spacesuit for
a MONKEY!

'Bat would look great in that,'
Maggie whispered to Arthur.

Arthur didn't reply. He and Freddy
had their hands up again.

'Yes, little buddy?' said Chuck to Freddy.

'Do astronauts poo in their spacesuits?' asked Freddy.

Everyone giggled.

'Um, well, maybe,' said Chuck.

Arthur waved his hand again and again, and finally burst out with, 'Some spacesuits have toilet bags in. But they have a special toilet on the rocket too.'

'But there's no gravity in space,' said Freddy. 'So all the poo would float out of the toilet!'

'That's why they're called "floaters"!' cried Matthew and burst out laughing.

'No,' said Arthur. 'The toilet has a vacuum that sucks up all the astronauts' poo.'

'You have to poo into a vacuum cleaner?' said Maggie.

'Well, sort of,' said Arthur.

'EWWWWWWW!'

went the class.

'Thank you, Arthur! I think we now know lots about space poo,' said Miss Raven. 'You can have ten house points.'

'Excuuuuuuuuuse me!' shouted Chuck. 'Are there any SENSIBLE questions about spacesuits?'

Isabella put up her hand.

'Yes?' said Chuck.

'How heavy is that spacesuit?' asked Isabella.

Chuck smiled. He knew the answer to that one! 'It weighs around 127 kilos or 280 pounds. It takes about forty-five minutes to put it on.'

'Wow!' said Freddy. 'How do the astronauts move about with such a heavy suit on?'

'Well,' said Chuck with a wink, 'that's why astronauts have to be so fit and strong.'

Arthur's hand shot up again.

'Yes?' said Chuck, through gritted teeth.

'They don't have to be that strong,' said Arthur. 'There's no gravity in space, so their spacesuits won't weigh anything. Which is good, because I want to be an astronaut and I'm not very strong.'

Chuck looked down at Arthur with a nasty little smile. '*You* want to be an astronaut, do you?' he said.

'Yes,' said Arthur.

'YOU can't be an astronaut,' said Chuck.

Everyone gasped.

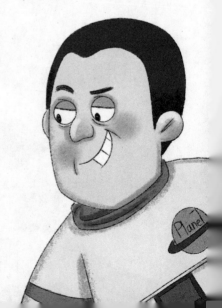

'Why?' asked Arthur.

'I thought *everyone* knew that astronauts need to have perfect eyesight,' said Chuck. 'And you do not. Sorry!' But Chuck didn't look sorry at all.

Arthur deflated like an unplugged bouncy castle. His eyes filled with tears.

Miss Raven had a "quiet word" with Chuck, before leading the class to the canteen for lunch.

Maggie hung back as the rest of her class trudged off.

'You shouldn't have said that to Arthur!' Maggie shouted at Chuck.

'Well, it's true,' said Chuck.
'Your little friend will never be
an astronaut.'

Maggie was furious! Her face
felt hot. Her fingers began to tingle
and tiny sparks started to fizz from
her hair.

As Chuck turned to walk away,
Maggie pulled out her magic wand,
gave it a wiggle and whispered:

'Magic wand from my back pocket,
make Chuck blast off like a rocket!'

POOF!

Chuck started to feel strange.
His tummy rumbled so much
that the ground shook.

Then with a great

WHOOOOOOOOOOOOOOOOSH,

he shot up into the air.

Chuck landed at the top of the rocket. He grabbed hold of the metal point and clung to it like a huge koala.

People gathered round and started clapping.

'Ooh!' said a little old lady to her husband. 'I didn't know the museum guides did tricks.'

The space centre manager pushed her way through the crowd and looked up. 'Colin Ramsbottom!' she shouted. 'Get down here at once!'

'I can't!' cried Colin (who had now forgotten all about his pretend name "Chuck"). 'I'm stuck!'

Maggie smiled. Then she tucked her wand away and hurried off to catch up with her class.

After lunch, crafts and a space-themed quiz, the science club headed back to the bus.

Maggie sat next to Arthur, but he didn't really want to talk to her.

'Take no notice of Chuck or Colin Bigbottom, or whatever his name was,' said Maggie. 'I think you will be a brilliant astronaut!'

'No, I won't,' said Arthur. 'My eyes don't work properly and I'm too small.'

Maggie tried to think of something to cheer him up. 'Arthur,' she said, 'if they let a monkey travel to space, I'm sure they'll let you too.'

'I want to be a proper astronaut,
not a **SPACE MONKEY!**' he said.

Maggie felt awful. She hated to
see Arthur so upset. She wanted to
do something to help.

Chapter 3

Back at home, Maggie told Mum all about her day – about how boring the rocks were, how Chuck (or Colin-whatever-his-name-was) upset Arthur and how astronauts poo into vacuum cleaners.

'What can I do to cheer Arthur up?' asked Maggie.

'I'm not sure,' said Mum. 'But he's very lucky to have a friend like you!'

'Why?' said Maggie. 'I don't know anything about space and I don't fit in with his science-club friends ... I don't fit in with anyone.'

'You don't need to fit in to be a good friend, Maggie,' said Mum. 'You care about how Arthur is feeling. You want to help him to

be happy. That's what makes you
a GREAT friend.'

'Thanks, Mum,' said Maggie.
Maggie did want to help Arthur to
be happy … but how? Maybe she
needed a little bit of MAGIC!

The next day was Saturday. Arthur's mum had a doctor's appointment, so Arthur came to Maggie's house for lunch.

He was still looking sad when he arrived, but Maggie had a feeling he wouldn't be for much longer. She hurried downstairs. A line of purple smoke was seeping out from under her bedroom door and her magic wand was still warm in her hand.

'Arthur!' cried Maggie. 'Come with me.'

Arthur trudged up the stairs behind her. When Maggie reached her bedroom door, she pushed it open and shouted, 'TA-DA!'

Arthur couldn't believe his eyes. He was in outer space!

The walls and ceiling of Maggie's room were black. Above their heads, a thousand stars, planets and comets (and a small chameleon-shaped astronaut) twinkled and danced about.

'Do you like it?' asked Maggie.

'It's ... it's ... wonderful!' whispered Arthur. He smiled for the first time in nearly two days.

'Oh good!' said Maggie. 'Since you can't go to outer space, I brought outer space to you.'

Maggie knew she had said the wrong thing when Arthur's smile vanished.

'No, I CAN'T go to outer space,' he said. 'And I really, *really* want to be an astronaut.'

Maggie flopped down on her bed, feeling hopeless. One star at a time, her bedroom turned back to normal.

Then, suddenly, she had a brilliant idea!

'You *will* be an astronaut, Arthur!' Maggie told him. She pulled out her wand again. 'I'll make sure of it!'

Maggie tried to make up a good spell. She couldn't think of anything that rhymed with "astronaut", so she gave her wand a wiggle and chanted:

'Turn Arthur with the gloomy face into someone from outer space!'

POOF!

'Oh dear!' said Maggie.

'What did you do, Maggie?' asked Arthur. 'I feel ... different.'

Arthur *was* different. His face was green, his ears were further away from his head and his fingers were much longer than before ... And he had an extra eye!

Arthur rushed over to the mirror. All three of his eyes opened wide in surprise. 'AAAAAAAAARGH!' he screamed. 'I'm an ALIEN!'

Arthur spun around. 'Look at me!' he said. 'My fingers are so long

… ooh! They light up at the ends. And look at my eyes – there's an extra one. Wow! I can see through your bedroom wall with it.'

'Really?' asked Maggie.

'Yes,' said Arthur. 'And your mum is running up the stairs!'

'Quick!' shouted Maggie. 'Hide!'

But it was too late. The door flew open and Mum burst into the room.

'Maggie,' said Mum. 'What's going on? I heard someone screaming. Where's Arthur?'

Maggie looked at the spot where
Arthur had been standing … but he
wasn't there.

'He's, er, hiding,' said Maggie.

'Where?' asked Mum.

'I don't know, Mum. We're playing "screaming alien hide-and-seek". I haven't found him yet.'

'Well, keep the noise down, please,' said Mum. 'Your dad is trying to write an article for the newspaper. It's not going well.'

'OK, Mum,' said Maggie.

'OK,' said Arthur's voice.

Mum looked around. She couldn't tell where his voice was coming from. 'Wow! Arthur really is good at hiding,' she said as she left the room.

'Arthur. Where are you?' whispered Maggie.

'Here,' said Arthur appearing
in front of her.

Maggie fell over in surprise.
'How did you do that?' she asked.

'I don't know,' said Arthur.
'I just wished I was under the
bed and WHOOSH, I was! Then
I wished I wasn't under the bed
and WHOOSH, I wasn't!'

'Wow!' said Maggie. 'I didn't mean
to turn you into an alien. But now
you have magic powers … you're just
like me!'

Maggie's smile quickly fell into a
frown. As cool as it would be to have
an alien best friend, she knew it wasn't
right. Arthur was a human. A human
with no magic powers, who was not
supposed to be "just like her".

'I'll call Grandad Sparks,' said Maggie. 'I'm sure he can change you back.'

'No! Not yet,' said Arthur. 'I want to see what else I can do. I want to try EVERYTHING!'

Oh no! thought Maggie. *Arthur has gone power mad!*

'I have not,' said Arthur. 'Hey, you didn't speak … I heard what you were thinking!'

This is so strange, thought Maggie.

'No, this is great!' said Arthur, who suddenly looked taller.

'Arthur, can you make yourself taller too?' asked Maggie.

'No.' Arthur laughed. 'My feet aren't touching the floor.'

'So you can–' started Maggie.

'FLY!' cried Arthur. He whizzed around the room like a big green bumblebee.

Maggie was worried. This wasn't what she had planned. *I must turn Arthur back to normal,* she thought.

'No!' said Arthur. And with a WHOOSH, he disappeared.

Penny the postwoman had just
dragged her post trolley all the way
to the top of the hill, when Arthur
suddenly appeared in front of her.
'Aaaah!' she screamed. Penny let go
of her trolley and it started rolling
back down the hill.

Arthur ran the other way, straight into a large group of people. Some of them took out their mobile phones and started taking photos.

Arthur could hear all their
thoughts. They were very noisy and
got all jumbled up in his head.

THE ALIENS HAVE LANDED!

What on earth
is that?

Arthur panicked. He ran down the street, round the corner and hid behind a large wheelie bin.

Arthur was scared. He wanted his mum. He was just about to wish himself back home when he remembered that his mum wasn't there. She was at the doctor's surgery, and he did not want to pop up there – not while he was an ALIEN.

What I really need is a friend, thought Arthur. WHOOSH!

CHAPTER 4

Arthur was suddenly back in Maggie's bedroom.

'Arthur! Thank goodness you came back,' cried Maggie. 'I've been so worried.'

'I'm sorry I left,' said Arthur, panting in panic.

Arthur was about to tell Maggie what had happened, when Maggie's dad burst out of his office. 'Hetty!'

he shouted. 'This is the story I've
been waiting for.'

'What story?' asked Mum.

'I've got to write it down quick,'
said Dad.

'I've got to send it to the national newspapers. I'm going to be famous. I'll be the first reporter to write about …
THE ALIENS LANDING!'

'Aliens?' said Mum lifting one eyebrow. 'Are you sure?'

'Yes!' Dad laughed. 'I've been sent photos to prove it!'

Mum picked Alfie up and went with Dad into his office. He was already on the phone to the TV news station when Maggie walked into the room.

'Er, Dad?' she said.

'Not now, Maggie. This is very important,' said Dad, holding his hand over the phone.

'But, Dad, there's something I have to tell you!' said Maggie.

'Well, if it's not about an alien

then it'll have to wait,' said Dad.

'It *is* about the alien, Dad!' said
Maggie.

Dad looked up just as Arthur
stepped into the room. Dad's jaw
dropped and so did his phone.

'Maggie, don't turn around. The ... the ALIEN is behind you,' he whispered. 'Just walk over to me veeeeery slowly.'

'But, Dad,' said Maggie. 'It's not an alien. IT'S ARTHUR.'

'It's me, Mr Sparks!' said Arthur, nodding so much that his third eye bobbed up and down.

'But, how?' said Dad.

'Magic,' said Maggie. 'I was trying to magic Arthur into an astronaut, but he turned into an alien instead.'

'I might have known,' said Dad, flopping down in his chair. 'The biggest story EVER and I can't even write it. If I did, everyone would know about us being magical.

We need to turn Arthur back to
himself. With a bit of luck, that will
be the end of it.'

But it wasn't.

'Tom!' said Mum. 'Look out of the
window.'

Dad peered through the curtains.
A huge crowd of newspaper reporters,
TV crews and police officers were
stood right outside of their house.

Mum handed Alfie to Dad and picked up the phone. She pressed the special star button that called a very SPECIAL person.

A moment later, with a loud POP and a puff of smoke, Grandad Sparks appeared.

'Hello, everyone,' he said cheerfully. 'Oh, hello, Arthur! You're looking a bit greener than usual.'

Maggie told Grandad Sparks what had happened.

'Oh dear,' he said when Maggie had finished. 'I'll need time to think about this.'

'There isn't any time,' said Arthur, using his third eye to look through the wall again. 'A police officer is coming to the front door.'

'Right!' said Grandad Sparks, rolling up his sleeves. 'This is going to take some serious magic. I need your help, Maggie!'

'What can I do?' asked Maggie. 'I can't do SERIOUS MAGIC!'

'You know Arthur better than any

of us,' said Grandad Sparks. 'I want
you to close your eyes and think
about everything that makes Arthur
special. Then hold my hand while I
say the spell. Arthur, you close your
eyes too – all three of them, please.'

Maggie took Grandad Sparks's
hand. She squeezed her eyes shut

and thought about her friend. All the
things she liked about him, even the
things that annoyed her. A WARM
feeling started in Maggie's chest. It
travelled down her arm, into Grandad
Sparks's hand.

Grandad Sparks raised his wand
and started to chant:

'Oh, little friend from outer space,
with googly eyes and bright green face.

Remember who you were before.
Turn back to Arthur Potts once more!'

POOF!

Arthur was back to normal! He
wasn't green, he had two eyes and his
ears were back where they belonged.
'Brilliant!' said Mum. 'Now,

Maggie, go and fetch your face paints.
We're going to turn Arthur back into
an alien.'

'What?' said Dad. 'We've only just–'

'Trust me,' said Mum. 'I've got
an idea.'

CHAPTER 5

Ding dong! went the doorbell.
Ding dong! DING DONG!

'Answer the door, please, Tom,'
said Mum. 'It'll be the police
officer.'

Dad walked down the stairs and
opened the front door. A large
police officer was standing on the
doorstep. Behind him was a big
crowd of people.

'Good afternoon, sir,' said the officer. 'We've had reports about an ALIEN outside your house.'

'An alien?' said Dad.

'Yes, sir,' said the officer. 'May I come in? I have some questions.'

'Of course!' said Mum, popping up behind Dad. 'Come in and have a cup of tea.'

The police officer walked into the hall just as Maggie, Bat and Arthur came running down the stairs. Maggie was dressed in her space witch costume. Bat was dressed as an astronaut. Arthur was an alien – well, sort of. He was covered in green face paint, had bright yellow washing-up gloves on his hands and he was wearing Maggie's alien eyeball headband.

'Hello, Mr Earth Police Officer,' said Maggie. 'I'm Maggie, the space witch, and this is Arthur. He's an alien!'

'BURBLE SPLINK!' said Arthur.

The police officer looked at Arthur and started laughing. 'And did you, little alien, go outside a short while ago?'

'NURDLE PLOOP,' said Arthur, nodding.

'He said "yes",' said Maggie, helpfully.

The police officer pressed a button on his radio and called the police station. He told them that the "ALIEN INVASION" was actually one small boy covered in green face paint.

Then the officer turned to Mum and Dad. 'I'll be on my way,' he said. 'I had better tell those reporters that the aliens haven't invaded after all.'

'What about your cup of tea?' said Mum. 'And you must try one of my scones.' Mum steered the police officer through to the kitchen.

'Can I have a scone too, please?' asked Dad.

'No,' said Mum. 'You have got an article to write … the true story of the alien invasion on Park Road. Finish it quickly, before those other reporters outside find out the truth too.'

Dad smiled and ran upstairs. By the time the police officer had finished his tea, Dad's story had been emailed to all the national newspapers.

DING DONG! went the doorbell again.

Mum opened the door to find Freddy, Tanek and Lily, with Tanek's dad hovering behind them.

'Hello, Mrs Sparks,' said Freddy.
'Is Arthur here?'

'Yes,' said Mum. 'Please come in.'

They all stepped in and gasped
in surprise.

'Wow, Arthur! You look brilliant!'
said Tanek.

'Why are you all here?' asked Maggie, sadly. Even though Arthur was dressed as an alien, she was starting to feel like the odd one out again.

'We found something we need to show Arthur,' said Lily.

The three children held out some photos of astronauts.

'I can't see anything special about them,' said Maggie.

But Arthur could. A huge grin stretched across his green face. 'Look, Maggie,' said Arthur. 'This astronaut is wearing GLASSES, like me. And this one isn't very tall

at all. If they can all be astronauts,
then maybe …'

'You could be one too!' said
Freddy, Tanek and Lily together.

Arthur looked so happy that
Maggie couldn't help but smile.

Maggie finally realised that
being different was not a bad thing.

It didn't matter that Arthur was small and wore glasses, and it didn't matter that Maggie was different from Arthur's other friends. She didn't need to "fit in". Being a good friend was all about helping each other to be happy!

'Hey,' said Maggie. 'We're playing space explorers. Do you want to join in? You can all be ASTRONAUTS!'

'Yes, please!' said Lily and Tanek.

'Do we have to poo into a vacuum cleaner?' asked Freddy.

'NO!' shouted Mum, Dad and Grandad Sparks together.

Continue the magic in ...

MAGGIE SPARKS

AND THE
FANG-TASTIC FAIRGROUND